This
Flashlight Night
belongs to

_____

(Write your own prayers on these pages.)

Flashlight Night

Elisabeth Hasselbeck

With **Grace Hasselbeck, Taylor Hasselbeck,** and **Isaiah Hasselbeck**

Illustrations by Julia Seal

That [Test] Will I play well
at School in the tournament?

My BEST
friend

NEW
Bike

(please!)

Will my
team WIN?

Come with me
and see this wall!
It's full of chalk
and super tall.

help
me
be
good

1
2

My friend who
is sick

they pick me?

Will I WIN the game?
Will I learn to blow a bubble?
Please h
That skateb d TRICK
The BIG Math Test
2x4
2x5
2x6
Staying out of trouble
Will I

It's where
I'm brave and
share my prayers . . .

my

biggest

hopes,

my
biggest
cares.

I hold some chalk
tight in my hand
and think and think and think
and stand.

With that piece
of chalk I write

with all my
HEART,

with all my
MIGHT ...

$\times 4 = 16$

My friend who just found out she's sick ♡ That Spelling test

That ☆ Skateboard TRICK

will I PASS the BIG Test? ✓

to shoes ☹

d who makes me feel so s

ey pick me?

The Big Math TEST

$4 \times 4 = 16$ HELP Wh

$3 \times 7 = 21$ na

$5 \times 8 = ?$

staying out of TROUBLE ☺

my friend who just found out

She's sick ♡ ☹ Will

All
that
keeps
me up
at
night.

Tie ny

Will I

Catch

the ☆

I learn to b a bu

Ball? 🏈

Can I

My **BIG**
math test,

catching
the ball,

that kid who
makes me feel
so small.

That I get all my
spelling words right,

that when
I'm mad,
I won't want
to fight.

You can write your prayers out too!

Here's some chalk for me and you.

You'll find it's easy once you start.

Share anything that's on your heart.

That skateboard trick.

The bike I want.

Our friend who just
found out she's sick.

Will I
learn to blow
a bubble?

Or tie my shoes?

Stay out of
TROUBLE?

At recess

be the

friend

they choose?

Multiply

and

divide

by twos?

$12 \div 2$

$10 \div 2$ $24 \div 2$

2×3 2×10

2×8 5×2

We sit and
look up at the wall.

Will our prayers be
way too **BIG?**

Or are they
way too

small?

One more thing—

I can't forget—

God, can You make me

kind of tall?

"You both are brave to write your prayers,"
Mom says with her bright smile.
"Let's give our worries up to God
and come back in a little while."

To us, a while feels like forever.

Actually, forever plus two!

Is that how long we'll have to wait

to see what God will do?

We wait and
wait and
wait to go . . .

Will the answers
be yes or . . .

no?

The waiting is done.
    The time is right.
Mom calls out,
    "It's flashlight night!"

Come on, friend.
Let's go see
what answers wait
for you and me.

Up
up
up
the
up
stairs

we climb
right to the spot:
the wall that holds
such special prayers,

some answered . . . and some still not.

"Do you see the wall?"
Mom asks.

"Yes, Mom,
I see it every
night."

She flips a switch and—*click*—
OUT goes the light.

"How about when it's dark?" Mom asks.

"Do you see it now?"

"I don't," I answer quietly,

"but I know it's there somehow."

"Now flash your light on the prayers
        where you see God's great big YES!
And turn your flashlight off
        where your yes has not come yet."

FLASHLIGHT ON!

I'm getting tall.

I've grown

an inch or two!

FLASHLIGHT OFF . . .

I'm still waiting

for a bike

that's red

and blue.

FLASHLIGHT ON!

I learned
to tie
my shoes.

FLASHLIGHT OFF . . .

That game
I play, I always
seem to lose.

FLASHLIGHT ON!

That boy who was
a bother is
now being nice
to me.

FLASHLIGHT OFF . . .

Our friend's still sick.

That skateboard trick
just gave me
a skinned knee.

FLASHLIGHT ON!
At swim class
I was really brave
and jumped
into the pool.

FLASHLIGHT OFF . . .
I still worry
about
the tests
at school.

Mom says, "Sometimes we see God's yes,
and other times we don't.
But just because it hasn't happened
doesn't mean it won't.

Even when it's dark and dim
and when we cannot see,
let's choose to place our trust in God.
He's close to you and me."

Dear God,

I'm thankful for a place to share
my worries, hopes, and prayers.
I'm thankful I don't have to fear
because You're always there.
I'm thankful I can trust You
with all my strength and might.
I'm thankful for family and friends
and for our flashlight night.

That Test at School
Will I play well
in the tournament?
My BEST
friend
NEW
Bike
please!
help
me
be
good
Will
who
is sick
help me

Psalm 56:3

"When I am afraid,
I put my trust in you."

Hebrews 11:1

"Faith is confidence in what we hope for
and assurance about what we do not see."

John 20:29

"Have you believed because you have seen me?
Blessed are those who have not seen
and yet have believed."

DEDICATED TO

Caroline, for being brave, taking my hand, and showing me your prayer wall.
You are an inspiration!

Rose, Percy, Elise, and Finn, for listening like young editors to these words on an airport floor.

Amelia and Louise. May this book bless you,
as your amazing book-loving mom made it happen!

All of our friends at Danita's Children in Haiti. We love you all the way from Nashville!

Jack, Charlie, Thomas, Therese, and all children out there who have
big wishes and prayers. God is listening!

Tim Hasselbeck, our strong and loving husband and daddy,
for always reminding us of God's presence.

FLASHLIGHT NIGHT

Scripture quotations are taken from the following versions: ESV® Bible (The Holy Bible, English Standard Version®), copyright © 2001 by Crossway, a publishing ministry of Good News Publishers. Used by permission. All rights reserved. Holy Bible, New International Version®, NIV®. Copyright © 1973, 1978, 1984, 2011 by Biblica, Inc.™ Used by permission of Zondervan. All rights reserved worldwide. (www.zondervan.com). The "NIV" and "New International Version" are trademarks registered in the United States Patent and Trademark Office by Biblica, Inc.™

Published in the United States by WaterBrook, an imprint of Random House, a division of Penguin Random House LLC.

WATERBROOK® and its deer colophon are registered trademarks of Penguin Random House LLC.

ISBN 978-0-525-65279-3
Ebook ISBN 978-0-525-65280-9

The Library of Congress catalog record is available at https://lccn.loc.gov/2020019147.

Printed in the United States of America

waterbrookmultnomah.com

2 4 6 8 9 7 5 3 1

First Edition

Book and cover design by Anna Bauer Carr
Cover and interior illustrations by Julia Seal

SPECIAL SALES Most WaterBrook books are available at special quantity discounts when purchased in bulk by corporations, organizations, and special-interest groups. Custom imprinting or excerpting can also be done to fit special needs. For information, please email specialmarketscms@penguinrandomhouse.com.